John Wager

Old Lane and Other Poems

Chiefly on rural subjects

John Wager

Old Lane and Other Poems
Chiefly on rural subjects

ISBN/EAN: 9783337424930

Printed in Europe, USA, Canada, Australia, Japan

Cover: Foto ©Andreas Hilbeck / pixelio.de

More available books at **www.hansebooks.com**

Old Lane and Other Poems,

CHIEFLY ON

RURAL SUBJECTS.

BY

JOHN WAGER.

——•——

LEEDS:
PRINTED BY EDWARD BAINES AND SONS.
1871.

"Come, see what pleasures in our plains abound :
The woods, the fountains, and the flowery ground."

VIRGIL.

"In those vernal seasons of the year, when the air is calm and pleasant, it were an injury and sullenness against nature not to go and see her riches, and partake in her rejoicings with earth and heaven."—MILTON.

"For I, that god of Lov 'is servauntes serve
Ne dare to love for mine unlikelinesse
Prayin for spede, al should I therfore sterve,
So ferre am I fro his helpe in derkenesse ;
But nathelesse if this may done gladnesse
To any lovir, and his cause aveile,
Have he the thanks and mine be the traveile."

CHAUCER.

PREFACE.

MOST of the following verses were written long years ago during the leisure intervals of a busy life in the industrial, and ever industrious, town of Leeds. From early days the love of nature and poetry has been to the Author a source of constantly recurring delight ;—inciting to rambles in the country among trees and flowers, green lanes, streams, and all lovely and peaceful things ; inciting also to free range over the noble heritage of poetic lore, which, accumulating through centuries, has made our Britain rich in treasures of thought beyond even the material wealth of its later days. But while, on the one hand, this love of nature and song has prompted in him also the endeavour to sing ; on the other, the knowledge acquired of the works of our great bards, and the deep appreciative reverence he bears for them, have sufficiently taught him that the world can very well spare the effusions of his lowly muse. Nor does he offer them to the world ; enough for him a few approving readers among the many thousand dwellers of his native town and neighbourhood ; and trusting that a faint spark of the heavenly fire has been granted, indulges the hope that when he lies mouldering in the grave some gentle lover of the good and beautiful—some toiler perchance in the murky town where himself long toiled, may now and then take up his unpretending volume, as he might pluck a random flower of the field, and feelingly recognize within it the impress of a spirit kindred and congenial with his own.

To several of the poems the date when published in sundry periodicals has been affixed ; especially to a few against which, from coincidence of thought or expression with works, high above his own, published after their first appearance, the charge of plagiarism against the Author might otherwise be made.

ABERFORD,
March, 1871.

Old Lane.

RIGHT dear art thou, Old Lane, so rough and rude,
    To him who, wrapt in self-communion sweet,
    Beneath thy leafy shade in solitude
Broods o'er his treasur'd thoughts ; or else doth greet,
With gladsome heart, the blackbird's shout of glee,
And throstle's lay of love, from some tall twisted tree.

Calm joy is his, and holy, tender feeling ;
    The world's vain hopes and fears alike forgot ;
His heart's own depths, and Nature's book revealing,
    Hints of that glorious world where sin is not ;
Down thy green path 'mid trees and wild flowers walking,
He feels his chasten'd soul with its own Maker talking.

Through leafy trunks, Old Lane, here many a time
    I've caught coy glimpses of the village spire ;
Heard the sweet music of its soften'd chime ;
    Lifting my spirit, like a hallow'd fire,
To purer raptures, to that holier place,
Where we, the veil remov'd, shall see Him face to face.

And how fond lovers love thy leafy shade !
    Where the warm whisp'rings of the simple heart,

Fram'd to sweet vows, so earnest, oft are made,
  And youth and maiden linger, loth to part,
Though fades the red light o'er the distant hill,
And in their cozy nests the weary birds lie still.

And dear thy rude old trees ! grotesquely dight,
  With palsied arms in netted ivy bound ;
In moss and lichens clad, grey, green, and white,
  Mark'd as with elfin language all around.
While high above them, on the quarry's brow,
Dark cloudy pines and tall light larches grow.

At intervals, with youth and beauty blest,
  A sylph-like birch bends o'er its silver stem ;
Woo'd by tall ash in graceful green robes drest ;
  And many a wild rose, deck'd with blushing gem,
Flirts with the bind-weed, and is quickly caught
In wreathed coils fantastically wrought.

And here and there a patch of broom and gorse ;
  Or rushy fen, or heath of purple glow ;
With asses grazing, or a lean old horse ;
  Or ragged lad, tenting a small Scotch cow,—
Spelling a book, perchance, but likelier seen
Flung vacant in the sun, or pelting newts I ween.

O, store with knowledge his untutor'd mind ;
  Quicken to life his undevelop'd thought ;
That, active and observant, he may find
  The teeming wonders by his Maker wrought ;
And may sweet visions bless his mental eye,
Such as young Nicoll saw when *he* " was herding kye."

Friend of the earnest, Nature, O impart,
   In this calm spot thy holy power to me;
Inspire my soul with wisdom, teach my heart
   Love like thine own, that henceforth I may be
A toiler in the ranks that nobly strive
To cheer all human hearts, all errors' chains to rive.

And, gracious God, the light of truth reveal;
   Each high resolve firm and effective make;
'That in luxurious dreams of human weal
   My spirit may not rest, but deep partake
Thy active virtue; nurs'd in loneliness,
But issuing forth elate the busy world to bless.

Once more, Old Lane, to thee: the peasant's cot
   Now passing by—rude-built, straw-thatch'd, and low;
'Mid orchard trees, and pleasant garden-plot,
   Where dainty flowers with homely pot-herbs grow.
"Tis eventide, the labourer's toil is done,
Smoking his quiet pipe he greets the setting sun.

And round about his prattling children prank,
   With ruddy health's impulsive spirits blest;
Or cautious peep where on the hedge-row bank
   The favour'd robin sits on mossy nest,
Hid by a primrose tuft—a needless shield;—
No child of grace would pluck a robin's bield.

Still struggling on, Old Lane, where dost thou end?
   Fain would I track each wild and pleasant nook;
Where plumy fern and blossom'd brambles blend;
   Where crazy bridges cross a shady brook,

That yields the water-hen a cool retreat,
'Mid rush, red willow-weed, rough sedge, and meadow-sweet.

But night's murk shadows gather round apace,
   Dimming thy wild charms to the outward sight;
Yet in my soul they have enrich'd a space
   With living pictures, fresh and sunny bright;
There to abide, and give, till being's close,
Pure tints of pleasure and serene repose.

1842

To the Violet.

OH, I would call thee sister, Violet!
 And, being poor, like thee be lowly-minded;
 Shunning the crowds enthrall'd in folly's net,
By fashion's glare and wealth's vain splendours blinded.

With anxious care thy own sweet virtues tending,
 Unmindful that no fame shall tell thy worth;
With calm content thy life in goodness spending,
 For its own sake—meek, modest child of earth.

In shady lanes deep-hiding out of sight;
 Blessing with fragrance grey decrepit trees,
That, muffled o'er with ivy, darkly bright,
 Nod their old heads fantastic in the breeze.

The peasant's children love thee, peeping round,
 Link'd hand in hand to find thee, purple gem;
And smile with joy, and kiss thy buds when found,
 Thou art so sweet, so passing dear to them.

Give me thy goodness, Violet, teach my heart
 The firm resolve to bless my fellow-man;
Nor slothful live, but act like thee the part
 Our God assigns in His eternal plan.

For what is life unblest with virtue's power,
　Or high or humble its possessor's lot ;
It fades away as doth a scentless flower,
　Loathing itself, unlov'd, and soon forgot.

But virtue does not die ; its memory sweet,
　In good men's hearts is shrin'd and cherish'd here ;
Its essence pure, for God's own garden meet,
　In changeless beauty blooms transplanted there.

To a Snail.

WHERE art thou roaming to, wonderful Snail,
　　With thy beautiful house on thy back ?
　　Outstretching thy soft horns, and leaving a trail
Of fine gauzy pearl on thy track.

Solemn thy progress, as if thou didst bear
　　The coffin and corpse of thy mate ;
And circumspect, feeling thy way with due care,
　　As becomes one who owns an estate.

A hermit, self-doom'd to prostration and peas,
　　In cold cell with no clothes on his back ;
A cosmopolite, ever at home and at ease ;
　　A poor pedlar, bow'd down with his pack.

The gipsy of Nature, unfetter'd and free,
　　Idly roaming the green earth art thou ;
Pitching thy tent in the lane 'neath a tree,
　　On the moor or the lone mountain's brow.

I meet thee at morn in my walk down the glade,
　　By the streamlet, or old hawthorn hedge ;
Tasting in quiet each delicate blade,
　　Or careering sublime on a sedge !

And I stop to examine thy elegant home
    With its chambers that wind up and down ;
All polish'd and smooth, like some porcelain dome,
    And enamell'd with white, red, and brown.

Beetle with bronzèd mail, grasshopper green,
    Bee, and butterfly splendidly bright,
May-fly, and dancing gnat—with thee are seen,
    And the glow-worms shine round thee at night.

In days of my childhood I've gather'd thy bields,
    And watched thy slow patient motion ;
Much musing if thou wert a native of fields,
    Or palmer foot-sore from far ocean.

Oft when the summer-blooms, beauteous, are gone,
    Scar'd away by the bleak wintry weather,
'Mong the dry leaves I find ye, or by an old stone,
    Like a hamlet cemented together.

Man, lordly man, discontented and proud,
    Lowly creature may gather from thee
A faith more sublime, and a heart calmly bow'd
    To the great Universal decree.

May learn to confide in that wisdom and might,
    That goodness unbounded and pure,
Which launch'd the vast suns in the ocean of night,—
    Gave the Snail a retreat so secure.

1843

Morning.

MORN brightens—the blackbirds shout loud from
the brake,
    The larks soar in rapture and sing as they fly;
Leaves glisten with dew-drops, the daisies awake
    And spangle the pastures like stars on a sky;
Brown hares in still woodland-walks sportively dally;
    Couch'd partridges, startled, wing whirringly by;
And soft comes the bleat of the lambs from the valley,
    And loud caw the rooks from their rude homes on high.

The cool east, enkindled, is glowing and blushing;
    Light clouds far and wide catch the rosy array;
Over lawns, lakes, and rivers the splendour is flushing,
    It burns the dim mist from the mountain away;
It ripples in gold o'er the wooded hill's host,
    Greets again the old tree that stands lonely and gray;
Then sweeps down the valley to meads it loves most,
    Where young men and maidens are tossing the hay.

Now strong through the minstrel's soul raptures are gushing,
    As he climbs to the dark rocky brow of the hill,
Where blooms the blue heather, and wild streams are rushing,
    And foaming and dashing in madness of will;
And soft steals the zephyr joy over his bosom,
    On green sunny banks where the streamlet is still;
Where the elfin bee wantonly rustles each blossom,
    And the glad heart of nature doth lovingly thrill.

1840

Lucy Bell.

"'Tis silly, sooth, and dallies with the innocence of love."

BY lofty mountains compass'd round,
 Within a silent dell,
Beside a tranquil lake is found
 The home of Lucy Bell.

A white-wash'd cot with garden'd front,
 With chimney round and strong,
And strong stone porch to bear the brunt
 When tempests scour along.

About the door and window-sill
 Thick clust'ring roses grow;
And pinks and pansies gaily fill
 Box-border'd beds below.

An elder-bush grows by the wall,
 The slates are tufted o'er
With golden moss; and over all
 Wide waves a sycamore.

Once on a pleasant morn in June
 I wander'd gay and free,

To list the woods' wild warbled tune,
  The sweet wild flowers to see.

By chance I saw young Lucy Bell
  Beside her mother's cot,—
Then blithesome birds and lovely flowers
  Were each and all forgot.

For not a flower, I lov'd so well
  Nor bird upon the tree,
Was half so sweet as Lucy Bell,
  Was half so blithe as she.

Her open brow was lily-fair,
  Her soft blue eyes were bright
As dew on violets; and her hair
  Did flow like wavy light.

I gaz'd upon her gentle face—
  A smile that gaze did greet;
But quick that smile did yield its place,
  Unto a blush as sweet.

That modest blush, that smile benign,
  That dear bewitching way—
My heart since then has ne'er been mine,
  She stole it on that day.

Invitation.

A SPRING DITTY.

COME, hie we to the woods, my Love,
  This sweet, warm sunny hour ;
    There rustling leaf and branch, above,
Our cool green walk embower :
And there for love the linnet sings,
  And bending blue-bells flower ;
There loving ivy climbs and clings
  Round oaks of lordly power.

Beneath, the rabbit frisks elate ;
  Aloft, the squirrel too ;
And they have each a happy mate
  To frolic with and woo ;
And deep among the leaves the dove
  Repeats his tender coo ;
And all things there, so happy, Love,
  Will welcome me and you.

Where blossoms of the hawthorn tree
  Delicious fragrance fling,
We'll sit and feel the sanctity
  Of loving hearts ; and sing
How love to life's thick, thorny brake,
  Sweet beauteous blooms can bring ;
And in each faithful spirit make
  A bright perpetual Spring.

Moonlight.

MAIDEN, lov'd-one, let us wander,
   See the solemn lamp of night
Over all the landscape yonder
   Sheds a dim and holy light;
Down the river richly streaming,
   Touching bright the rocky steep;
Broadly o'er the forest gleaming,
   Where the mighty shadows sleep.

Dreamy, dim, serenely cold,
   Nature, in a tranced mood,
Deep communion seems to hold
   With the soul of solitude;
Earth is silent, stars on high
   Silently the earth survey;—
(Each with calmly raptur'd eye)
   Marching in sublime array.

Deep the silence, yet a sound,
   List intensely, you will hear;—
Far within the vast profound,
   Mingled music, sweet and clear;
Spirit-voices, soft and low,
   Hymning in that realm above,
Where the founts of being flow
   In perennial streams of love.

Maiden, thus with thee for ever
  Fain would I be doom'd to dwell ;—
Gazing on the moonlit river,
  Up the dim, mysterious dell ;
Mystic mood, from Nature caught,
  With our blended spirits blending ;
Wrapt in love and lofty thought,
  Pure, sublime, and never-ending.

To Nature.

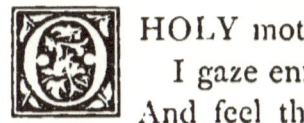 HOLY mother! with deep calm devotion
  I gaze enrapt upon thy beauteous face;
 And feel the glow of grateful warm emotion
When I remember all thy tender grace,
Thy constant care, the admonitions mild,
Through life extended to thy lowliest child.

How thou hast led me gently by the hand
 To clearest streams, through greenest meadows gliding;
Sweet flowers hast shown me, and tall trees so grand;
 And birds that sing thy hymns, and birds' nests, hiding
Their freckled treasures in dark leafy bow'rs;
And all fair wondrous sights in this fair world of ours.

And as my years increas'd with me did range
 Through cottaged dales in softest charms excelling;
Didst fire my soul with impulse wild and strange
 On dark huge mountains, far from human dwelling;
And with vast wonder and absorbing awe
When ocean's waves, wide welt'ring, first I saw.

Nor this alone; but gradual led'st me on,
 Through charmed sense, to that mysterious seeing

By which the soul, sublim'd, can gaze upon
　　The kindred soul of universal being;
Can feel in mountain, sky, in river, tree and flower,
A presence bright with love—a vast pervading power.

And taught my heart to love each living thing;
　　And most of all to love my fellow-man;
To seek sincere for truth and to it cling,
　　Spite of the worldling's sneer, the bigot's ban;
By self respect supported—that high mood
Born of free, earnest thought, habitual rectitude.

And bade me, silent, wait on the Divine;
　　The solemn teachings heed for evermore
Of its pure spirit, whisp'ring unto mine;
　　In woods and hallow'd groves to bend before
The sacred altars of the dread Unknown,
The Central Life unseen, through all life ever shown.

Oh, holy Mother! plant the wise and good,
　　(That thou mayst love me still) deep in my heart;
That wand'ring forth o'er mountain or through wood,
　　Thy spirit may be with me, and impart
The peace profound, that pure and lofty joy
The world can give not, neither can destroy.

Sabbath Days.

"Sweet day! so calm, so cool, so bright,
The bridal of the earth and sky."—HERBERT.

THANK thee, God, for Sabbath days,
  Those blessed days so cool and bright,
When labour rests, and grateful praise
Fills wearied hearts with calm delight.

A heavenly peace from purest sky
  Blends with all earthly sounds and things,
The flowers' still smile, the zephyrs' sigh,
  Seem tender, holy worshippings.

I hie me to an ancient place,
  With belfry small, among the trees;
Where simple hearts, refined by grace,
  Feed chaste and hallow'd sympathies.

In that small temple, lowly lone,
  How softly song with music blends;
How hallow'd, deep, the whisper'd tone
  Of reverential prayer ascends.

C

Earth seems forgot; faith, hope, and love
   Lend to the spirit glorious wings,
And, gazing with meek eyes above
   She towards her high appointment springs.

And full of peace the Sabbath eve,
   When ling'ring sunbeams lengthen day;
Like angel visitants that leave
   A blessing ere they pass away.

A blessing dwells in thoughts sublime
   That stir the soul's deep silent stream;—
Far-stretching past the bounds of time,
   Where vast, unutter'd glories beam.

And felt through all the heart—refined
   By nobler passions, pure desires;
By love which burns for all mankind,
   And, soaring to its source aspires.

Toiling through life's perplexed maze,
   Man were devoid of noblest worth,
But for these constant sweet relays,
   These precious hours of heaven on earth.

But the vast love which feeds each creature,
   Gives the field flower its bright array—
Hath granted man's immortal nature
   That richer boon—the Sabbath Day.

May.

JOYOUS May, the free and fair,
    Comes to bless the earth again;
  Flushing all the balmy air
  With the glory of her train;
Dropping flowers of every hue,
Gold and purple, red and blue;
Thrilling thousand hearts with gladness,
And a rich and lofty madness,
    And a soft delicious pain.

Sunshine woo's the green and gold
  Of the mighty forest tree;
Flower in conscious beauty bold
  Smiles its smiling mate to see;
Cloud for cloud hath rosy glances;
Stream to streamlet prattles, prances;
Gorgeous fly its consort chases
Over all luxurious places,
    Lightly laughing at the bee.

O'er the rooks' ancestral grove
  Floats a loud and loving sound;
And the skylark, mad with love,
  Plunges in the blue profound;
While humbler birds their passion tell
Amid the copse wood in the dell,

And shepherd lads their lassies woo
In woodland walks, where ringdoves coo,
    And bending blue-bells deck the ground.

Mystic web of antique story,
    May's sweet magic can unfold ;—
At her touch a crimson glory
    Decks the gnarl'd crab, sere and old ;
Ragged hawthorns start to sight
Robed in rich embroider'd white ;
And the brown and blasted moor
Groweth green, and blazes o'er,
    Effulgent with the gorse's gold.

Month of beauty, love, and pleasure !
    Carking cares be cast aside ;
Trending to some ancient measure,
    Let us wander far and wide ;
Bringing back with heartsome glee
Blossom'd trophies from the tree,
Every bloom that pranks the Spring,
To wreathe for May a votive ring,
    As in England's early pride.

In her brief, bright golden days,
    Song and music be combined ;
Let the poet chant her praise,
    As, on mossy bank reclined,
He, the beating pulse of Nature,
Shares the joy of every creature ;
Loveth all things—sun and shade,
Bird and flower, and rosy maid—
    Like the Universal Mind.

Autumnal Sunset.

HOW rich and deep, when day departs, the sun's autumnal beaming,
   O'er all the grandeur of the earth celestial glory streaming ;
O'er all the full munificence that loads the teeming sod,
Diffusing far a gorgeous light—the smiling of a god.

Bright beaming on the distant rocks' bold, bare, projecting brow,
That bask reflects the radiance o'er the bosky glooms below ;
And glowing rich on crimson bells that deck the moorland hills,
And teeming molten gold among the waters of the rills.

The huge oak lifts his hundred arms to catch the glory bright,
And maiden birches bathe their hair amid the beauteous light ;
It pierces through the dusky pines, thick-mass'd with bristling wire,
And glares beyond as if all space was one vast furnace fire.

On mingled woods, so richly dight, green, orange, red, and brown—
Proud swelling over hill and dale—the glory teemeth down ;

On sprightly deer in parks it shines, on calm domestic herds,
On simple sheep, composed for sleep, on home-returning
    birds.

O'er waving seas of precious corn a benediction flinging,
As joyous reapers, wending home, their even-song are
     singing;
On luscious fruit in orchard-grounds the streaming splendour
    comes,
On meadows green, brown fallow fields, on round, red clover
    blooms.

It floods o'er wooded pastures wide, and loit'ring milkmaids
    see
Long lines of shadow stretch away from every scatter'd tree;
And far up green, o'ershadow'd lanes, quick shoots a
    quiv'ring ray
To quiet, dim, secluded walks, where raptured lovers stray.

It burnishes the window-panes of stately pillar'd hall,
And smiles upon the dying rose by peasant's cottage wall;
It strikes upon the village-spire and tips it with a star,
On city domes and pinnacles—bright flashing from afar.

And thus it shines o'er many a land, and distant nations gaze
Upon the vast magnificence, now passing, in amaze;
And many a kindred spirit feels a joy sublimely great
While wand'ring forth this eventide alone to meditate.

And thus it shone in days of old, when holy prayers were
    said,
And vesper song was sweetly sung in pile now mouldered;

Through windows dim and beautiful with soften'd power it
 came,
Commingling like the soul of God with rapt devotion's flame.

And it will shine divinely bright, as future ages roll,
On millions blest with peace and love—the sunshine of the
 soul;
All disenthrall'd from vice and want, all happy, wise, and
 good;
A wider. Eden won again, a boundless brotherhood.

Now slowly down the west descends the glorious orb of
 Light,
By cloudy grandeurs compass'd round, that burn intensely
 bright;
Then, streaming rays of glory far, it passes from the eye,
But with a rich and golden glow suffuses all the sky.

Then deeper hues of gorgeousness come gradual o'er the
 scene,
And saffron pale, and purple, dim the gold and crimson
 sheen;
The eastern sky grows cold and blue,—there starlets faintly
 shine;
While o'er the west huge shadows stretch, like giants laid
 supine.

They deepen yet—to sadder hues slow changes all the sky,
And gleams of red and lurid gray wild intermingled lie;
Till all the rich magnificence is pall'd and lost to sense,
Yet leaves on lonely traveller's mind a solemn influence.

 1839.

The Approach of Winter.

(Written on a Stormy Autumnal Day.)

THE harvest time is past, and now
    The shadow of a scowl,
That chills fair nature's genial glow,
Falls from approaching winter's brow;
A gloom hangs over all below,
    And sinks into the soul.

Along the hills the weeping cloud
    Its mourning garment trails;
The autumn winds sigh deep and loud,
Dead fallen leaves the streamlet shroud,
Dark alders moan, the ash is bow'd,
    The stern, strong oak-tree quails,

The golden glory of the year
    Grows dim and wanes away;
Brown stubble fields look lone and drear,
The draggled fern is sad and sere,
And darkness like a passing bier
    Looms o'er the short-lived day.

The flowers are deadly sick and pale,
    Fast fading to the tombs;
The jaded bee's chill'd efforts fail,
The birds are silent, but a wail—
A funeral moan—sounds on the gale,
    Sad through the twilight glooms.

I feel a strange mysterious dread
  Creep o'er me where I stand;
I hear low voices of the dead,
Unearthly music overhead,
And tortured groans of ghosts that tread
  Down to the darksome land.

The wild waves on the river shore
  Like human life rush past;
They plunge and fret, they roll and roar,
In trouble tossing o'er and o'er;
But urged onwards evermore
  They reach the goal at last.

O! sad to think that all fair things
  Fade like an evening sky;
The flower that blooms, the bird that sings,
The blush on beauty's cheek that springs,
The hopes and joys life's morning brings,
  Must sink again and die.

The Spring comes forth with buds and shoots,
  Gay Summer brings the rose;
And loving life sweet life salutes,
And pleasure blends with bold pursuits;
Then Autumn brings the ripen'd fruits,
  And Winter brings the close.

Thus wheel the circling seasons round,
  And thus the year of man:
For him one Spring to till the ground,
One Summer's suns for growth abound,
One ripening Autumn only found,
  One Winter seals the plan.

To Melancholy.

COME to me!
O come to me, ethereal influence,
Absorb my spirit, trance my waking sense,
'Mid solemn cedar groves, with silent eloquence.

O come to me!
Come thou to me where murkiest shadows fall
From ivied masses of old abbey wall,
At dumb, dark midnight—heaviest hour of all.

O come to me!
In mid profound of vast primeval wood,
When sere leaves madden in the whirling flood
And voices speak—awful, dim-understood.

O come to me!
On loneliest beach dark dreary ocean laves,
When billows welter, and the wild wind raves,
Or mournful howls through dank and dismal caves.

O come to me!
At sunset come when distant wood and wold,
Floating in gorgeous seas of vapoury gold,
Mysterious visions seem, which airy sprites unfold.

O come to me!
O come to me with most sweet pensive pain,
When lonely music's far-off vesper strain
Is heard, then dies—is heard, and dies again.

O come to me!
When golden sheen has faded all away,
And hills and valleys, pall'd in livid gray,
Grow mute as death, and yield to night's dark sway.

O come to me!
When cold, pale moonlight's calm and languid beam,
Sleeps on lone heath, still lake, or scarce-heard stream,
With hallow'd, death-like, dim, Elysian gleam.

O come to me!
Come, chiefly come, when one lone star shines bright,
Fill me with sweet sad fancies—dreamy, light;
Glide often down those beams of earliest night.

O come to me!
Bless me for ever! may I distant be
From haunts of men, with vision-shapes and thee;
Sweet, lonely pleasure feel—pure beauty's essence see.

Beckhay Banks.

(ABERFORD.)

ON Beckhay Banks the birch-tree grows,
   Pale ash, and dusky pine;
   The harebell decks their shaggy brows,
  Wild rose, and columbine;
And by the burn, on bosky brae,
The linnet sings there all the day.

At rosy morning, cool and bright,
  I've walked their woods between,
And gazed around, from craggy height,
  On meadows fresh and green;
On sailing cloud, and azure sky,
And uplands wooded gorgeously.

At noon, beneath the beechen tree,
  Beside the mossy well,
I've sat in dreaming fantasy,
  Enthrall'd by fairy spell;
Or reading Spenser's antique page,
Or Wordsworth, high, poetic sage!

And oft at evening's quiet hour
  I've mused beneath their shade;

When dying winds, and water's power
  Have soothing murmur made :
In holy meditative mood,
The luxury of solitude.

O rare the bliss that Nature yields
  Her ardent votaries,
Who woo her in the yellow fields,
  'Neath vernal, sunny skies,
At pleasant prime of flowery May,
When Love and laughing Joy have sway.

Or seek her spirit, more sublime,
  Where rocks tremendous frown ;
'Mid solemn forest shades, what time
  The leaf is sere and brown ;
And awful thoughts, and feelings grand,
Sweep o'er the soul at her command.

For Nature in deep silent speech
  With man can sympathise ;
Can renovate his heart and teach
  His spirit to be wise ;
And therefore still with spirit meek
I would her holy altars seek.

1841.

Troutbeck.

LONELY valley, lying sweet and green
'Mid mountains proud to compass such a scene;—
The Yoke, Hill Bell, and High Street over all,
A huge and massive, dark, impending wall,
To check barbarian storms that issue forth
From outer regions of the gloomy north;
And keep the valley aye serenely blest,
And calm and holy as a hermit's rest;
Calm as its own pure church that meekly stands,
Hinting of God, amid the harvest lands
And waving woods—that join the gushing river,
'Neath its white walls, in solemn chaunt for ever.

O sweet to trace this river, as it rushes
'Mid mossy rocks, through tangled roots and bushes;
Passing quaint cottage and sequester'd mill;
Like child of genius with a wayward will,
Silent and darkling now, now flashing free,
Tossing and tumbling with intensest glee;
Loit'ring in nooks where Spring begins her pranks,
And with the earliest primrose decks the banks;
Bids lady-ferns on lowly violets tend,
And troops of lilies in white robes descend;
Flings *ladies' smocks* and *bedstraw* for the fairies,
And, like our river, full of wild vagaries,

Up the green hill-side trips, so light and fleet,
With *Ragged Robin* and *Meg-many-feet*.
Then, down returning, joins our joyous stream
That plunges sudden—startled from a dream—
Through Thwickem's copses, Calgarth's ancient woods,
On to the ocean of our mountain floods,
Mighty Winander, that serenely lies
In the calm glory of the evening skies.

More grand to trace its upward source sublime,
'Mid dripping clouds, and mountains black with time;
Through gloomy caves, aud huge rocks rent asunder
By wedge of winter's ice and crash of thunder;
Through the deep hollow where in ages past
The frighted Briton hid in forest vast,
While high above the conqu'ring Roman strode,
And paved on topmost ridge his level road.
Passing the *Park* where erst in days of old
A mighty giant dwelt, Hugh Hird the bold;
Who single-handed stood in grim array,
And drove invading Scots another way,
Flinging huge trees at every breechless elf—
A mighty catapulta in himself!—
Long ere auld Hoggart whipp'd the wicked ways
Of village *statesmen* in his rustic lays;
Ere Adam Walker taught the dale to know
How cabbage sprouts and tails of comets grow;
Or Sally Birkett, famed through all the glen,
Brew'd stalwart ale for nose of mortal men.
Then up we rise to Kirkstone dark and drear,
A fortress held by Winter all the year;

Where the great painter, Martin, once did stand,
And, prophet-like, saw visions vast and grand ;—
Gleams of bright heaven above the rolling clouds
And hell's abysses 'neath their murky shrouds,
As from deep gulfs the black rocks rise and pass
Their jagged summits through the seething mass ;
Hereafter fix'd with pencill'd power sublime,
For admiration of all future time.

Blithe are thy daughters, Troutbeck, fair of face ;
Tall and large-limb'd thy sons, a hardy race,
Upon the rugged fell-side feeding sheep ;
For wrestling famous, and the daring leap.
And oft erewhile in brunt of battle tried,
Their country's glory proving, and her pride ;
Worthy of those whose arrow-heads did glance
Fierce lightning flashes in the fields of France ;
Worthy of those who in these later days
At Balaclava won immortal bays.

But, lovely vale, of war I will not write,
But rest my pen where mingled woods invite
To rocky seat ; and listen with a tear
A sweet, sad ditty to the dying year,
Sung by the lonely robin from a tree ;
While, in most strange and solemn symphony,
Wave with soft sighs the birks and ashes pale,
And weeping clouds look sad, and winds and waters wail.

October, 1860.

To a River.

SPORTIVE Young River, we've rambled together
Over the mountain-moors, purpled with heather;
On, where the fox-glove and bracken wave over
The blackcock and curlew, the pewit and plover:
And down the rough rocks with a shout of delight,
Where the wild elfin birches are dancing in white;
And onward again with a sparkle and splash
To the dank dusky woods of oak, alder, and ash;
And down deeper still to the green sunny valley,
With frolic and laughter, with song and with sally.

Beautiful River! full many a day
In that green happy valley we've saunter'd away,
Watching the flight of the light cloudy shadows,
Listing the low of the kine in the meadows,
The chirp of the grasshopper, hum of the bee,
And sweet loving song of the bird on the tree;
In a world of our own, without sorrow or sin,
All peaceful around us, all peaceful within;
While gay pleasant fancies, profuse as the flowers,
And musings and calm meditations were ours.

True-hearted River! there came a sweet rill,
Fresh as the morn, from a neighbouring hill;

D

And ye kiss'd, and united, and flow'd on in one,
O'er rugged and gentle, through shadow and sun ;
And I found a sweet maid in a nook by thy side,
Where bees, birds, and roses enraptured abide ;
And glad was my heart as the soft summer breeze,
As we whisper'd and walk'd 'neath thy bowering trees ;
And that young lovely maiden, so modest, benign,
Is the rill whose pure being is blended with mine.

Strong-hearted River, undaunted and free,
Rejoicing in labour, I've labour'd with thee ;
And felt thy glad spirit expand in my heart,
While humbly, but earnestly, filling my part
In the plan of the universe—best understood
While working with all things together for good ;
While manfully striving and gathering strength,
Through patient endeavour, to triumph at length,
And win the high guerdon, and learn the deep lore,
Unfolding to true earnest work evermore.

Majestic old River ! we're passing away
From the land of our pilgrimage, green and gay ;
Ample and deep thy beneficent course
Calmly rolls on to its primitive source ;
While I lonely listen the low solemn sound
Of that ocean, more awful, no shingles surround ;
Dark bourne where the streams of all life and time tend,
All thought, love and hope, joy and sorrow descend ;
And I pray, as I bow to the fiat divine,
For calmness, and courage, and strength like thine.

1849.

To the Skyrac Oak.

HUGE leafless skeleton, grim, gaunt and old!
    Lifting thy jagg'd arms to the sky defiant,
    Like blasted body of some Titan bold—
Struck and transfix'd when time was fresh enroll'd,
    Fierce warring with the gods.—O, forest giant,
Though black and shatter'd, sapless, dead, and cold,
    I gaze upon thee with blent awe and wonder;
For thy vast life hath braved the storm and thunder
From ages dim, remote;—when Hedda stood
    And pierced the red deer on the trackless moor;
    When angry wolf snarl'd at the bristling boar;
And Loidis was a hamlet in the wood
    That joined to Sylvan Elmete—waving grand,
    One wide umbrageous forest o'er the land.

Fragment.

LONG have I lov'd, with deep and earnest truth,
    The soul of Nature; from my earliest youth
    Roaming in rapture through dusk woodland alley,
Deep bosky dingle, broad luxuriant valley,
O'er heathy moorlands, 'mid rude rocks and streams,
By lonely meres and mountains,—till my dreams
Were wondrous Edens, and all pleasant places
Haunted my memory like familiar faces.

The Woods of Croft.

I N sweet spring-time, when leaves are young,
　　And hearts are warm and soft,
　Upon my arm blithe Margaret hung
Within the Woods of Croft.

　　O, merrily coo'd the stockdove,
　　And merrily sung the thrush ;
　　And merrily trill'd each tiny bird
　　On every bank and bush.

We wander'd here, we wander'd there,
　Through all the pleasant valley ;
Through meadows green, by river-scene,
　Through every woodland alley.

　　O merrily flicker'd the sunshine,
　　And merrily blew the breeze,
　　And merrily danced a myriad leaves
　　Upon a thousand trees.

With jest and joke, and pleasant speech,
　All joyous as the weather,
We sat beneath a spreading beech
　And carv'd our names together.

O merrily bloom'd the primrose,
And merrily curl'd the fern ;
And merrily peep'd the speedwell,
Beside the bosky burn.

Her hand I clasp'd, and, O divine !
  I snatch'd a tender kiss ;
Sweet Meg, I said, wilt thou be mine ?
  And Margaret answered—Yes.

    Then merrily, merrily sung the birds,
    And merrily piped the breeze ;
    And merrily, merrily danced the leaves
    Upon ten thousand trees.

Song.

FAIRER to me is the cheek of my Love,
    Brighter to me is her bonnie black eye,
      Than the fairest of flowers that bloom in the grove,
  Than the brightest of bright stars that spangle the sky.

The pure thoughts of her soul softly beam in her face !
    The sweet smile which is there tells her goodness of heart;
Intelligence, modesty, truth, wit, and grace,
    To her form and her features their treasures impart.

If I did not love her I should not love heaven,
    For she is the semblance of those that are there ;—
An angel of light to mortality given,
    To teach us to worship the good and the fair.

Sisters.

SISTERS, word of tenderest might!
　　Exciting blissful recollections;—
　Sweet childhood's hours, so soft and bright,
So simple, earnest,—such delight
　　Of gentle young affections.

Flowers of the hearth! as tender, fair,
　As though to *please* your sole vocation:
Yet hearts you have, and souls, to bear
Life's earnest duties, roughest care,
　　With cheerful animation.

Men are there who did ne'er behold
　A lovely sister's smiling face:
I pity them, so stern and cold,
Their hearts unsoften'd, uncontroll'd,
　　By beauty's pure refining grace.

Young sisters, with their play and prate,
　To please in merry fit;
And older ones, serene. sedate,
To soothe, instruct, or recreate
　　With music, taste, and wit.

Ah ! gladsome evenings spent erewhile,
　Around the parlour table,
With tale, and song, and merry smile,
With pencil, pen, or pleasant wile
　Of books of quaint old fable.

Ah ! sweet days past, in summer's pride,
　'Mid sunshine, birds, and buds ;
By flowery streams where minnows glide,
Where screams the jay, and berries hide
　Cool in the leafy woods.

And yet, though rare we take our places
　'Neath that paternal roof ;
Though time hath touch'd some slighter graces,
We love "the old familiar faces,"
　The records of our youth.

And hope, as years their circles move,
　For many a happy greeting ;
For kindly acts, and cordial love,
And when life ends, in heaven above
　One other glorious meeting.

1844

The Home of Taste.

"Give him a home—a home of taste."—ELLIOT.

Y Margaret, our lowly home shall be a home of taste,
A sunny spot to nestle in amid the "streeted
waste;"
Though round our door no cool green grass, no cheerful
garden grows,
The window-sill shall blossom with geraniums and the rose.

Our parlour wall all up and down, for moral and delight,
We'll hang with pleasant pictures, of landscapes green and
bright :
Of portraits of the wise and brave, the deathless sons of man ;
And love to teach for all that live the good Samaritan.

Of Burns, too, and his Highland Maid, much lov'd, lamented
Mary ;
And by its side that *aged* pair whose love no time could vary ;
For love, up-welling pure and deep, from youth to sober age,
Shall be a light and blessedness through all our pilgrimage.

And the drawings that you drew at school, for the joy that
in them lies,
The memory of our early life when earth was paradise ;
And I'll sketch the ruin'd priory, by the river, dim and gray,
Where wrapt in love's delicious dream we linger'd many a day.

A goodly bookcase we will store with learning's precious
    gold—
A hallow'd temple to enshrine the mighty minds of old ;
Deck'd with a bust of Shakspeare, and one of Milton too,
And when my work is done, my Love, I'll sit and read to
    you

Some thrilling tale of olden time—love true in evil day ;
Some loftiest song of holiest bard, some gentle minstrel's
    lay ;
Or wondrous revelation of science deep and high,
Or Christian theme, that we may learn in peace to live and
    die.

And we'll not forget your music, love, the songs so sad and
    sweet,
You sung to me with a tearful eye in your father's calm
    retreat ;
And oft that music of the heart we'll sing it o'er again,
And link our days together still with its enchanting chain.

Will not our life be happy, Love ? O yes, for we will seek
The spirit of the Spotless One—the beautiful, the meek ;
All pure desires and high resolves, all lofty thoughts and
    true ;
And that which duty bids be done our willing hands shall do.

Will not our life be happy, Love ? O yes, for we will bow
Together at the throne of Him " from whom all blessings
    flow ;"
And deep in His eternity—beyond the change of time—
And deep within our inmost soul, enjoy a peace sublime.

A Day Dream.

THE land I love is not a land
    Of mountains capp'd with snow ;
    Of boundless plains where rivers grand
Through boundless forests flow.

It is a land where uplands green
    Slope gently to the sun ;
And little streams, the hills between,
    Their quiet courses run.

Where crops of oats and lentils grow ;
    Where barley braves the breeze ;
And golden wheatfields richly glow
    Against the green of trees.

Of pastures broad where lazy sheep
    Grow fat and fair in clover ;
Of thymy knolls where you may sleep
    In moss half-cover'd over.

Of snug warm cots with rose-wreath'd walls,
    That shelter rosy girls ;
Of homesteads with their thrifty halls
    Well-stock'd with British churls.

The maid I love she is not one
  With outward charms resplendent;
Whose flashing eyes reveal a sun
  Of intellect transcendent.

And yet she hath a pleasant look,
  Like sunshine on green fields;
While treasures rich as any book
  Her noble nature yields.

She hath a true and loving heart;
  A firm but gentle mind;
With hands that to her household part
  Are cheerfully inclined.

For she all arts of woman's place
  Hath made her special care;
Can run a seam with nimble grace—
  The neat repast prepare.

And yet can read with feeling tone
  The poets high creation;
On painting gaze, or sculptured stone,
  With true appreciation.

A song can sing that pity moves,
  Or glads this life of ours;
And much I love her that she loves
  The holy life of flowers.

The day is fix'd, the blessed day,
  That seals this maiden mine;

Henceforth through life's perplexed way
   A guiding star to shine.

A star of hope—through years to come
   With minor orbs surrounded ;
All moving in the heaven of home,
   By love's horizon bounded.

All moving on, as day and night
   And time glide calmly past,
With bounteous warmth and cheerful light
   To set in peace at last.

A Word for Water.

HE sprightly lark that soaring high,
Rings sweet alarums through the sky;
And countless choristers that throng,
At his high peal to matin song;
And thrill through every sacred grove
The wild ecstatic notes of love,
Of nature's bounty take their fill
And sip refreshment from the rill.

Th' untiring beasts whose useful toil
Prepares the fructifying soil;
And those more fierce that darkly prowl,
Through tangled woods with savage growl;
Strong limbs and mighty hearts have they,
Yet nature's simple laws obey;
She gives them life-sustaining food,
And purest draught from crystal flood.

Through all her vast domains below,
She bids the limpid wave to flow;
But man in his inventive pride
Her simple cordial has denied;
And mix'd himself a cup of pain,
The fatal draught that fires his brain,
Pollutes his blood, corrupts his heart,
And dims the bright, immortal part.

On Enquiry

Being made respecting the Religious Opinions of the Writer
by one disposed to make his acquaintance.

ASK not what your creed is, man,
  Why make you quest of mine?
'Tis very simple in its plan,
  And yet, I think, divine.

I do believe that God the blest
  Loves all—both Turk and Jew,
Son of the Pope, and Methodist—
  That are good men and true.

No cold stone wall, no thorny fence,
  No privet, neatly grown,
Can keep his blessed influence
  Exclusively your own.

And he most godlike is on earth
  Whose loving sympathies
Can see and own true moral worth
  In every mental guise.

Song.

FAINT heart never won fair lady,
    Never lofty guerdon gain'd ;
Bear thy spirit calm and steady,
    On the true path unrestrain'd.

As the great sun, cloud-invested,
    Burns and wrestles with the spell,
Till scatter'd hosts of gloom detested
    Far and wide his triumph tell.

So with earnest, firm advances
    Battle in the mortal strife ;
Till all adverse circumstances
    Show the lustre of thy life

Aphorisms.

Sinful life, sad parting breath;
Holy living, happy death.

March to thy labour right cheerfully, man,
Work is the good God's beneficent plan.

From the Danish.

Well-born is sure a guerdon bright,
    And better still well-bred;
Well-married is a life's delight,
    But best of all well-dead.

From the Swedish.

The goods which sin hath gotten with sorrow go again,
But righteously-acquired wealth with honour doth remain.

E

To Religion.

O SAY, blest Spirit, deign'st thou but to dwell
    In Gothic dome, whose grand expansive height,
    Dimly illumed with gorgeous-colour'd light,
Sounds with the slow and deep-toned organ's swell?
Amidst the splendour of long-vista'd aisles,
    Where pomp and pride, and wealth and power abound,
Dost thou alone dispense thy heavenly smiles,
    And shed thy power, divinely calm, around?
Nay, rather, where the poor man meek and good,
    With wife and babes in lowly peaceful cot,
Bow down to thank their Maker for their food,
    And all the blessings of their lowly lot,
Delightest thou to dwell, and there dispense,
Unto these humble ones, thy soothing influence.

Devotion.

I.

HOW fair are flowers, blue skies, clear rills in motion!
Yet fairer a Young Maiden at devotion,
In reverential silence.   Her rapt spirit,
(With God communing, seeking to inherit
All hallow'd thoughts, each lovely, pure desire),
Illumes her features with such sainted fire,
That as we gaze unseen we feel a solemn awe
As we some holy one—some bright immortal, saw.

II.

What awful grandeur dwells 'mid mountain forms.
Or robes itself in sunset, clouds and storms!
And yet, more grand an Old Man bow'd in prayer,
Deep, holy, calm.   Thin locks of long gray hair
Wave lightly round his temples; grief and time
Have scath'd his ample forehead—sad, sublime;
Yet o'er these rugged lines a softening grace,
Sweetly benignant, beams around his face
Like an encircling glory.   Feeble though his frame,
His soul is strong in love, and hope's unfading flame.

Incitement.

WASTE no time in wishes vain,
    Or retrospective sorrow;
  Work, and hope will spring again—
Joy return to-morrow.

Yon darksome cloud that fix'd as death
    Doth seem to sorrow's eye;
A slow but mighty moving breath
    Is heaving from the sky.

Lo, even now through rifts of blue
    The gleaming light appears;
Like holy eyes soft smiling through
    The solemn veil of tears.

All earnest, truthful work is blest;
    Ask Nature's laws to aid thee;
Then work and wait, and trust the rest
    To Him above who made thee.

WAIFS.

Enigma.

I'VE three feet on short legs, but without any toes;
A very wide mouth and a very long nose;
Like the grim ghost in Hamlet I come in the night,
Clad in helmet and corslet of steel shining bright;
By nature I'm rough, yet a polish acquire;
My temper's not bad, though it often takes fire;
Although without wings, I can take a bold flight,
And eagle-like soar to the source of the light; '
I drink not, though dry, but eat while I'm able,
And cram myself oft till I'm sick at the table;
Of tobacco I nowise encourage the trade,
Yet indulge much in one thing that from it is made.

ANOTHER.
(TO A LADY.)

YOUR tears I share when sad at home,
    Like constant friend and true;
    I press your lips; and when you roam
    I take the air with you.

Yet oft for this a storm you vent
    Of angry huffs and blows,
Till quite incited to resent
    I nip you by the nose.

Then peace succeeds, and it may hap,
    So fickle is the fair,
You place me gently on your lap
    And let me slumber there.

Clovelly.

A QUEER little place is Clovelly,
  But likely long time to keep good;
For partly 'tis pickled in brine,
And part kept like wine in the wood.*

Ilkley Well.

L ADY, why hangs that lovely head,
  Like a rose-bud bent with dew?
  "Alas! kind sir, the flames of love
Have pierced me through and through."

Then take a plunge in Ilkley Well,
  'Twill cool you, will it not?
"Ah, Doctor, no—love's heart would make,
  The water boiling hot."

---

* This picturesque Devonshire village consists chiefly of one narrow street, or alley, which clambers most irregularly up a steep hill-side; with its lowest houses laved by the sea, and its highest overshadowed by trees on the summit of the cliff.

To Miss Black.

(A BEAUTIFUL YOUNG LADY OF REMARKABLY PALE COMPLEXION.)

LADY, your face so lily-fair,
    So spotless, pure, and bright,
    Confounds my senses, and I swear
In raptures, Black is white.

From a Bachelor to a Lady

Who had sent him a fragment of Bride-cake to "dream upon"
by placing it under his pillow.

THE potent charm of sugar'd-cake
    I placed beneath my head,
    And an awful dream made my soul to shake
As alone I lay in my bed:
A fairy thief so bland and blithe,
    Came smiling where I lay
And open'd my *chest* with her fingers lithe,
    And carried my *heart* away.
And again I dreamt, that the very next night
    She came so blithe and bland—
But I woke in a sweat and a terrible fright
    For the robber was *taking my hand!*

Epitaph

ON AN IDEAL PHILOSOPHER.

BENEATH this stone at rest lies one
(Removed from life's rude clatter)
Who was pure spirit while he lived
And when he died no *matter*.

On the Death of Toby,

A PET PUG.

POOR Toby's dead! in sad array
Lament with sorrow sore;
Alas! he died but yesterday,
And never died before.

But woful friends let tears be dried;
One joy doth yet remain,
Though Toby dear dog, once hath died
He'll never die again.

The Supremacy of Goose.

OF all the fowl of field and fen,
    Of coop, or wood, and water,
By cruel cooks and gentlemen
Predestin'd to the slaughter,
There's none I swear that can compare
With an old gander's daughter!

The Distracted Lover.

COULD he fix upon the *fair*,
    Chloe thou wert sure his choice,
For thy beauty's passing rare;
    But thy sister's silver voice
Draws his spirit unaware;
    And from thee he turns away
    To list, enchanted, to her lay.
    Yet when 'tis o'er his eyes return,
    Like moths, within thy light to burn;
    And thus 'tis his perplexed fate
    Between the two to oscillate,
    And like the learned Schoolman's ass
    Amid abundance starve, alas!
    Were she dumb, or were he blind,
    Then firmly could he fix his mind.

A Conjecture.

(SUBMITTED TO CLASSICAL SCHOLARS.)

JOVE'S council o'er, the gods so bright
　Would lay aside the crown,
And recreate in soft delight,
Strong nectar quaff with main and might,
　The cares of state to drown.

But since we find their race is o'er,
　I have just now been thinking,
That they, poor gods, like many more,
Had topers turn'd, and tumbled o'er,
　And kill'd themselves with drinking.

The Blacksmith:

A BALLAD,

Which showeth the Efficacy of the Cold Water Cure.

B EN Burnwind was a blacksmith bold,
    With arm of mighty sweep;
And in his better days, I'm told,
    Three journeymen did keep.

But he, alas! from love of drink
    Lost all his worldly pelf,
And sick at heart did often think
    That he would hang himself.

Yet flashing fits of joy he found
    In his most deadly bane,
And as the luring cup went round
    Resolv'd to live again.

Thus wretched, self-abhorr'd, through life
    He dragg'd full wearily;
Ne'er human wight had woe more rife,
    Through all the earth than he.

Stung with remorse he sometimes said,
    With heavy heaving sigh;
"Ah! where shall I go to when I am dead!
    For a sinful man am I."

And fancy oft, with fearful glance
　In midnight's awful gloom,
Saw fiery eyes and horns advance
　To fetch him to his doom.

It came to pass, one close of day,
　In a state of intoxication,
Reeling about, he chanced to stray
　To a Temperance Convocation.

A pale thin man was holding forth
　The worth of water pure—
The new-found saviour of the earth,
　The universal cure !

His lavish praise, so fast and free,
　Flow'd forward like a flood,
That some a deluge thought would be
　Much for the public good.

Doctors henceforth might whine and weep,
　And drink their drugs themselves ;
And parsons with their *Fathers* sleep
　In dust upon the shelves.

For it would cure diseases foul
　When unadulterated ;
And Satan ne'er would fetch the soul
　With water saturated.

And men would live as fresh as fry
　Of river-fish in May ;
And of extreme age scarcely *die*,
　But gently glide away.

Deep sunk his earnest argument
  In Ben's bemuddled mind,
Who pond'ring said, as home he went,
  "Nought else will do I find."

And so, to where the river roll'd,
  Not waiting for the morrow,
He turn'd and took a plunge-bath cold
  That ended all his sorrow.

NOTES.

TROUTBECK, p. 36.

Foremost among the famous men of the small but beautiful vale of Troutbeck, near Windermere, Westmoreland, stands Hugh Hird, the giant. Besides the redoubtable encounter with the Scotch rebels recorded in the poem, he is celebrated throughout the length and breadth of the land for another marvellous feat, which occurred at the building of Kentmere Hall : namely, that of lifting unaided into its place, six feet high, a huge beam, thirty feet long, which twelve men had previously attempted to raise, and were not able to move. Once upon a time also he went to London to wrestle before the king. On arriving at Court, being asked what he would like to eat, he replied, "the sunny side of a wether ;" so when his meaning became known, the royal cook roasted a whole sheep, and Hird ate every bit of it, bones excepted, declaring he had not had so good a dinner since he left home. We may be sure that he did not meet with his match in the wrestling ring ; and when he came away the king was so well pleased with his exploits that he made him a grant of the half of Troutbeck Park—then an unreclaimed wilderness covered with large trees. The gift, however, proved fatal ; for so impatient was the giant to clear it that he killed himself with the violent exertion of pulling up the trees by the roots. Tradition says that he was the child of a nun ; but an entry in the parish register records the baptism of a Hugh Hird, son of William Hird, on the 20th of September, 1609. This would bring the heroic ages of Troutbeck down to recent times.

Another of the Troutbeck worthies, Thomas Hoggart, the rhymster, commonly called Auld Hoggart, was born in the village, and died there in 1709. He was uncle to Hogarth, the great satirical painter ; and with vastly inferior genius, possessed a somewhat kindred spirit, which prompted him freely to castigate, in rhymes sometimes coarse enough, the follies and vices of his neighbours. He wrote also several play-gigs, which according to a letter, by Adam Walker, in the *Gentle-*

man's Magazine, were performed by himself and his rustic associates, in the open-air at Troutbeck, in a wonderful manner and with wonderful success. A picturesque old cottage which once belonged to the family is still known in the village as Hoggart's House.

Adam Walker himself ranks among the noted men of Troutbeck, having been born there about the year 1727. In his day he enjoyed considerable reputation as a lecturer on natural philosophy, and published a book on the subject of the lakes; beyond this, little respecting him is known.

More conspicuous in the annals of the dale is the name of Julius Cæsar Ibbetson, who about fifty years since resided in the village, and is yet remembered by a few of its oldest inhabitants for his gay eccentric habits, jovial countenance, rotundity of nether person—of such a fulness that he could scarcely stoop to the ground—and, above all, as the painter of the famous signboard that gave name and immortality to the Mortal Man. On this tablet of the inn which since at least has borne this singular name, he depicted, it is said, with amusing caricature the portraits of two of the Dalesmen—Nat Fleming and Ned Partridge—strikingly contrasted in physiognomy and frame; the one jolly, rubicund, and rotund as himself; the other lank, lean, and pale-visaged as a ghost. Beneath, the following verse was inscribed :—

> "O, mortal man that liv'st by bread,
> What is it makes thy nose so red?
> Thou silly fool, that looks so pale,
> 'Tis drinking Sally Birkett's ale."

When its owner quitted the inn he took the signboard with him; the price demanded for it being refused, and it has probably ceased to exist.

The highest dwelling-house in England stands within the township of Troutbeck, on the summit of the Kirkstone Pass; and here a painter of still wider fame, the sublimely imaginative John Martin, spent a summer in careful study of the grand and desolate scenery by which he was surrounded; and here he also painted a signboard, representing the Pass and the humble hostel in which he dwelt. For awhile it did public service effectually over the door; but being also depreciated by a new tenant, and eventually purchased by a Kendal gentleman, it retired into private life.

The *statesmen* (estatesmen) of Troutbeck were formerly far more numerous than at present; the late aged incumbent had heard an old friend say that in his early days the valley was owned by seventy proprietors—now reduced to about thirteen. The younger sons of these

F

yeomen frequently entered the army, and especially the corps of life-guards, which received no inconsiderable number of recruits from the tall, hardy, and vigorous natives of this and the contiguous dales. Even now, when the number of tall men is said to have diminished, not a few in Troutbeck are six feet and upwards in height. A native of the valley was recently champion wrestler of England; and another frequently won the prize for leaping at the athletic contests held periodically in the neighbourhood, and formerly presided over by the late Professor Wilson. Instances of vigorous longevity occur amongst the Dalesmen; one of them when upwards of eighty-four years of age could on occasion walk thirty miles a day; and Margaret Longmire, who died in 1867, in her 104th year, plied her knitting needles almost to the last.

THE SKYRAC OAK, p. 41.

This venerable relic of the primitive forests of Old England stands in the pleasant village of Headingley, near Leeds, bearing a superscription which declares it the original oak from which the wapentake of Skyrac was named; as, however, there is no evidence of the truth of this assertion, it is well that time has almost effaced the inscription, and wreathing ivy concealed the tablet on which it appeared. Thoresby seems to have been the unwitting source of the statement, by the expression of a mere conjecture which he founded upon the pre-eminent size and age of the tree, and the circumstance, "that in the wapentake or subsidy rolls, Headingley led the van rather than towns more considerable in other respects." But, as Dr. Whitaker observes, a district so extensive would in those early times abound with thousands of large oaks, each as likely to have been the tree in question; and he adds, that a wapentake court, about the end of the thirteenth century, was actually held for Skyrac between Garforth and Manston.

Nevertheless, if the patriarch of Headingley has not given name to the wapentake, it was probably co-temporary with the oak that did; and being now indisputably the oldest sylvan inhabitant of the district, has legitimate right to the name of the Skyrac, or Shire-oak, which the wapentake may be regarded as having conferred upon it. Not very long ago, however, it had a rival, or at least a compeer, in the field; for the writer has seen a sketch, by the late J. N. Rhodes, of another

"Huge oak, dry and dead,"

which stood somewhere in the neighbourhood of Headingley at the time when the sketch was made.

The trunk of the old tree, which is quite hollow, measures twenty-one feet in circumference at a yard from the ground; in the school-days. of the writer it bore foliage, but its stag-horned branches have long since shed their last leaf. More than twenty years ago the principal bough then remaining fell off, but a portion of it I hope yet survives in the form of a handsome writing desk which its timber supplied. Ivy planted about the same time at the foot of the tree, has mounted to its summit and thickly mantled its dark and rugged trunk, imparting to the grandeur of its age somewhat of the grace and beauty which doubtless blended with the vigour of its earlier years.

The custom of assembling for public purposes under great trees, and especially beneath the oak, is of ancient date. Our ancestors, Celtic and Teutonic, like the Greeks and Romans, held the oak sacred—worshipping in oaken groves; and for ages afterwards some lingering sanctity brooded amidst the umbrage of its leafy boughs. Wonderful to the Briton were the virtues of misletoe that grew upon the oak; in Germanic forests a huge oak was worshipped as a God; down to the thirteenth century the states of East Friesland assembled under three large oaks; beneath an oak that long bore his name, Augustine preached successfully to the pagan Saxons of Kent; Edward the First held a council under the Parliament Oak in Nottinghamshire; the Oak of Reformation waved its approving arms over Kett the Tanner as he told assembled serfs and villeins that they ought to be free men and receive wages for their work; and ages before the old Moot Hall rose at the foot of Middle Row, in the toiling turmoiling town of Leeds, the *gemote* of its wapentake was held, it appears. under or around some great Skyr-ac, or municipal oak-tree.

The sub-division of a county called a Wapentake is the same as that of a Hundred; as the term is peculiar to those northern counties which were especially Danish in their population, it is supposed by some to have been introduced by the Danes; but whether or not, the custom from whence the name is derived certainly accords with the ancient Scandinavian mode of confirming the election of their chiefs or kings. namely, by the touch or clash of the weapons of the people assembled at their Thingsteads in the open-air. Among the Anglo-Saxons a wapentake (like a hundred) consisted of ten tithings, each composed of ten families; it was so called because the chief of the wapentake (high constable of the present day) on being appointed to office appeared on horseback at the customary site with a spear in his hand, and was there met by the principal men of the wapentake, who by *tac* or touch of his *wapen*, or weapon, with theirs acknowledged his authority and agreed to give it their support. The hand-stroke by which country people, in England and Scandinavia, confirm a bargain or agreement is a similar custom, transmitted no doubt from those early times.

The etymology of Headingley is by consent of Thoresby and Whitaker, the Field of the Son of Hedda; Heddeing, and Son of Hed, being regarded as synonymous terms. "Who this Hed was," says Thoresby, "or the name of his son, I will not pretend to discover at the distance of so many ages, their memory being lost, with innumerable other places and persons famous in their generations." As, however, *ing* also signifies a pasture or meadow, and Hed is Danish for heath, it is quite possible (Yorkshire abounding in Danish terms) that Heding may, like Hatfield, mean nothing more than heathfield, or moorfields, with *ley* (similar in meaning to *ing*) for an addition of later date.

Thoresby contends that Loidis (Leeds), and not Lincoln as some have it, is the British *Caer Loid Coit* (City in the Wood) mentioned by Nennius; possibly, however, the name may have some affinity with the Anglo-Saxon word *leod*, people; as well as with the names of two hamlets near Aberford, called High and Low Leod, or Led. The Regis Loidis, or territory round Leeds, mentioned by Bede, is supposed by Thoresby to be identical with that of Elmete; but he confesses himself quite unable to define its bounds. Berwick-in-Elmet, and Sherburn, concerning which Lombard's dictionary, published in 1577, says—"The territory or Hundredth about Skyrburne in Yorkshire is called Elmete," give some indication of its extension to the east; how far it extended in other directions is matter of vague conjecture only, the word Elmet, so far as now known, not having attached itself to the name of any other place. Of the extent, however, of the district some hint at least is found in a M.S. quoted by Camden, which states that Elmed-Setna (population of Elmet) occupied 600 hydes of land; but the hyde was not a fixed and uniform measure throughout England, and the quantity of land the term anywhere expressed is not now exactly known; being indefinitely stated at as much as could be ploughed with one plough, or as much as would suffice for the support of one family, and variously estimated at from sixty acres to more than double that amount. Mr. James, in a paper read some years ago before the Archæological Society, considers that 600 hydes would in the north be equivalent to much more than 136 square miles; and states also that we cannot be certain that Elmet when the M.S. was written retained the full extent of its earlier bounds when it formed a small independent British state. That such a kingdom as

Elmet existed here long after the Saxon invasion, hemmed in by Saxon sovereignty on every side, appears evident. Its population probably consisted of Britons of Deira who had found shelter in the great forests of the district; and partly favoured by the nature of the country, and partly perhaps through sufferance and forbearance, disturbed occasionally by Saxon encroachment, held independent possession of the tract till Edwin became King of Northumbria, about the year 617. One of the earliest deeds of this monarch, Lappenburg informs us, "seems to have been the conquest of the little British territory of Elmet, which had existed as an independent state under its king Cerdic—a name susceptible both of a British and Saxon interpretation—whom he expelled, for having under the guise of hospitality, received and afterwards poisoned Hereric, the nephew of Eadwine, who, like his uncle, had been persecuted by Ethelfrith." The same author supposes that Elmet was connected with Cumbria, then a British region which included the present Cumberland, Lancashire, and Westmoreland; having its several kings, who, however, were sometimes united under a pendragon or supreme chief. In the paper previously referred to it is conjectured that the area of this little state embraced the valleys of the Aire, Wharfe, and probably Calder too; that Leeds was its capital; and that Farnley Wood near Leeds, Bishop's Wood near Sherburn, and other ancient woody tracts, are vestiges of the great forests that harboured the Elmet Celts.

It is rather singular that while Deira, Bernicia, and other states have transmitted their British appellations this little kingdom which kept its independence so long should be distinguished only by a Saxon name. Yet such is the case, if as Thoresby affirms, the name is derived from the great woods of elm which then and long after abounded here. "The word Elmet," he says, "means frondolous, full of branches, as the country then doubtless was, like a continuous shade or grove by the interweaving of the branches." Many instances occur of local names derived from the elm, in Saxon lands both at home and abroad: as Elmham, a town in Norfolk, and Elmshorn, a village in Holstein; but the word may with equal plausibility be derived from a man's name, or the alder tree, as from the elm, if instead of Elm-ete we read El-mete— the mete or boundary of El. The alder is yet abundant over the supposed area of Elmet, and, delighting in moisture, would be still more so before the river margins of its valleys were embanked, and its numerous carrs were drained. This surmise derives support from the fact that while there are few, if any, places within or about the district named after the elm, there are many that bear the name of the alder in one or other of its dialectic forms. Æl, Al, El, Elle, Eller, Oller, and Owler, are variations of the name of this tree, most of them common both to Yorkshire and Scandinavia; and evidently showing that it has given name to Alwoodley, Allerton, Ellerton, Ollerton, and Elslack: probably to Hellefield and Helwick, and other places within or close on the border of the district assigned to Elmet; as well as to *Elleskov* and *Ellemose*, alder-wood and alder-moss, in Denmark; and to *Elsbruck*, alder-waste, in Germany, where Frederick the Great won a battle.

The venerable Bede informs us that Paulinus, after the conversion in 627 of Edwin the great Northumbrian king, "built a church at Campodonum" (supposed to be Doncaster), "which afterwards the pagans by whom king Edwin was slain, burnt, together with all the town, in the place of which the later kings built themselves a country seat in the country called Loidis; but the altar being of stone escaped the fire, and is still preserved in the monastery of the most reverend abbot and priest, Thridwulf, which is in Elmete wood." The situation of this monastery has been variously assigned to Berwick-in-Elmet, Tadcaster, and other places, but where it actually stood is unknown. From the above passage it would appear that the Regis Loidis (country of Loidis) and Sylva Elmetæ (Elmete wood) were not, as Thoresby supposes, co-extensive and the same; or at least that Elmete wood was a more circumscribed locality than Elmete itself; and this has been taken for granted in the sonnet on the Skyrac Oak.

EDWARD BAINES AND SONS, PRINTERS, LEEDS.

www.ingramcontent.com/pod-product-compliance
Lightning Source LLC
Chambersburg PA
CBHW030018030726
47499CB00008B/3043